THE CASE OF THE
HALLOWEEN GHOST

HANK THE COWDOG.

THE CASE OF THE HALLOWEEN GHOST

· John R. Erickson ·

Illustrations by Gerald L. Holmes

Maverick Books
Published by Gulf Publishing Company
Houston, Texas

10 9 8 7 6 5 4 3

Maverick Books
Published by Gulf Publishing Company
P.O. Box 2608 Houston, Texas 77252-2608

Hank the Cowdog is a registered trademark of John R. Erickson.

Book and cover design by Tom Hair.

Library of Congress Cataloging-in-Publication Data
Erickson, John R., 1943–
    The case of the Halloween ghost / John R. Erickson; illustra-
tions by Gerald L. Holmes.
        p. cm.
    At head of title: Hank The Cowdog.
    "The ninth exciting adventure in the 'Hank the Cowdog' series"—
    Summary: Hank the cowdog has one of the scariest adventures
of his life when he and his cowardly companion, Drover, find
themselves in a strange and spooky place on Halloween night.
    ISBN 0-87719-148-4 (hbk.).—ISBN 0-87719-147-6 (pbk.).—
ISBN 0-87719-149-2 (cassette)
    1. Dogs—Fiction. [1. Dogs—Fiction. 2. Halloween—Fiction.
3. Mystery and detective stories. 4. Humorous stories. 5. West
(U.S.)—Fiction.] I. Holmes, Gerald L., ill. II. Title.
PS3555.R428H286 1990
813'.54—dc20
[Fic]   90-13583
                                                              CIP
                                                              AC

Printed in the United States of America.

To Kris on our 20th anniversary

Have you read all of Hank's adventures?
Available in paperback at $6.95:

All books are available on audio cassette too!
($15.95 for two cassettes)

Also available on cassettes:
Hank the Cowdog's Greatest Hits!

Volume 1 Product #MB4120	$6.95
Volume 2 Product #MB4137	$6.95
Volume 3 Product #9194	$6.95

Contents

Contents

CHAPTER 1

THE MYSTERY BEGINS WITH SOMETHING FISHY

It's me again, Hank the Cowdog. Slim's house was cold and also a terrible mess, and I haven't gotten to the part about the ghost yet.

There's a reason for that. A guy can't get his entire story into the first paragraph, no matter how hard he tries. So you'll just have to be patient. I'll get to the part about the ghosts as quick as I can. And when I do, you'll probably wish I hadn't.

What we've got cooking here is one of the scariest stories of my entire career, mainly because it involves a GHOST. I didn't think I believed in ghosts, but as you'll soon see, the ghost we encountered didn't really care whether I believed in him or not.

So there you are.

It all began, mysteriously enough, at the beginning, and I happen to know the exact time it began: around six o'clock on the evening of October 30.

Drover and I had been making a routine patrol around the western quadrant of ranch headquarters, when all at once we encountered Pete the Barncat down at the calf shed.

There was nothing particularly mysterious about that, because the calf shed was one of his favorite loafing spots. He had several favorite loafing spots. He loved loafing above everything except himself.

Have I ever mentioned that I don't like cats? I don't like cats, Pete in particular. So when I saw him primping and preening himself there by the calf shed, I slipped up behind him, said "WOOF!" real loud, and gave him a good scare.

Ho, ho. Hee, hee. Ha, ha. I love it!

He turned wrongside-out, hissed, gave out his usual "Reeeeerr!" and climbed the nearest post.

"Sorry, Cat, but we don't allow loafing or loitering on this outfit. If you'd been taking care of the mouse problem, I wouldn't have had to do that."

2

He glared down at me with his big cat eyes. "Oh, it's only Hankie."

"Yeah, and Drover," said Drover.

"I thought maybe it was a ghost."

"A ghost?" said I. "Not likely, Cat. I run a tight ship here and I don't allow ghosts on my ranch."

G.L.Holmes

"Oh really? Did you know that tomorrow night is Halloween?"

"No, I didn't know that. Now ask me if I care."

"Mmmmm, all right. Do you care?"

"Not even a little bit. But, for the sake of argument, what is Halloween?"

Pete moved off the post and parked himself on the top board of the fence. Funny, how a cat can do that. "Halloween is the scariest night of the year. It's the night when all the ghosts and goblins come out."

"Oh my gosh," said Mister Scared-Of-His-Own-Shadow, "I don't think I'll like that!"

"Quiet, Drover. I'll handle this." I turned a withering gaze up to the cat. "For your information, Kitty, we don't observe Halloween on this ranch, and if you run into any gobs or ghostlins, you might tell them the same thing."

"It's *ghosts or goblins*," said Drover.

I stared at him. "What?"

"I said, ghosts or goblins."

"Yes? Is that supposed to mean something?"

"You said 'gobs or ghostlins.'"

"I did not."

"Did too, I heard you."

"And so did I, Hankie." That was the cat. "You said 'gobs or ghostlins.' But no matter

4

what you call them, they'll be out tomorrow night because tomorrow night is Halloween, and you can't stop it from being Halloween."

I drew myself up to my full upright position. "Oh yeah? I said there will be no Halloween on this ranch, and *there will be no Halloween on this ranch,* period."

"Oh yes there will, Hankie, because Halloween is already on the calendar."

"Oh no it isn't, Kitty-Kitty, because I don't believe in calendars, ghosts, goblins, or Halloweens, and as long as I'm in charge of Ranch Security, what I believe is the definition of what IS. Any more questions?"

The cat smirked down at me and twitched his tail. "When you see the ghosts and goblins tomorrow night, remember these words: 'Wlcidkgh elskck clslckbnnbe slckeke.' "

"Huh?" I turned to Drover. "What did he just say?"

"I don't know."

I turned back to the cat. "What did you just say?"

"I said, 'Wlcidkgh elskck clslckbnnbe slckeke.' "

Must have had some wax in my ear, couldn't make a lick of sense out of what that cat was saying. "What?"

"Come closer and I'll say it one more time."

I hopped my front paws up on the fence and . . . you know what that sneaking, no-good, counterfeit . . . he slapped me across the nose with his claws, stung like fire, brought tears to my eyes, and before I could hamburgerize him, he had vanished.

Drover was staring up at me. "What did he say, Hank?"

"He said . . . shut your little trap and get back to work, you nincompoop, you've just been duped by the cat."

"That sounds like something *you* might say."

"I just did."

"I thought maybe you did. But what about Hollereen?"

"It's been cancelled."

"Oh good! Are the ghosts cancelled too?"

"That's correct. Come, Drover. We've used up our allotment of time for your bungling and now we've got work to do." We headed east, out of the front lot and into the saddle lot, and ran into Slim. He had just finished his chores and was closing up the medicine shed for the night.

Drover and I fell in step beside him and escorted him to his pickup, even though my nose still hurt. He lived in a little hired man's house down the creek—Slim did, not my nose; my nose lived on my face—and he was fixing to drive home for the night.

The sun was going down in the . . . well, in the west, of course, and a chill was beginning to rise from the ground.

Slim blew on his hands and rubbed his arms and looked down at us. "Why don't you boys come home with me tonight? I need some company, and I'll let you stay inside."

Stay inside, like your ordinary pampered house mutts? No way. In security work, we've got to be just a little . . .

Oh what the heck, one night in a nice warm house . . . we hopped into the pickup and headed down the creek.

After all, Slim needed company. He was lonesome and . . .

Okay. We pulled up beside the house, after a bone-chilling ride in the back of Slim's pickup. Drover and I were near frozen, yet somehow we mustered the energy to leap out of the pickup and make a lightning dash for the front door. We were shivering, see, and ready to begin our evening of selfless volunteer work around a nice warm wood-burning stove.

Slim pushed open the door and we raced inside.

Drover cheated and got there first. When I arrived, he had seated himself in front of the wood stove. I went over and joined him, although sitting in front of the stove didn't do either of us any good because the fire had gone out.

Between shivers, Drover looked around the living room and said, "Gosh, I wonder what happened to this place." It was a mess.

"I'm not sure, Drover. Either a train wreck or tornado."

Slim came over and dropped an armload of wood beside the stove, pitched his coat over the back of the nearest chair, opened up the stove, shoveled some ashes into the ash bucket, made a little teepee out of kindling wood, and started wadding up newspapers and pitching them inside.

Then he lit a match and before long the stove was blazing and the chimney was roaring. He closed the door and held his hands over the stove.

"There. Now we've got us a fire." He walked into the kitchen and built himself a sardine and ketchup sandwich for supper, and

I, being the senior member of the crew, took the best spot, right in front of the stove.

Say, it was really roaring and kicking out the heat now. Felt wonderful. Sent warm delicious waves up my backbone and out to the end of my tail.

My eyes began to droop and I entered into a state of near perfect contentment—until Drover broke the spell.

"Hank, do you smell something?"

I sniffed the air. "Yes. Sardines."

"Do they have kind of a burned smell?"

"Negative. Sardines are a species of fish, son, which explains why they have a fishy odor."

"That's funny. I thought I smelled burned hair."

"Impossible. Sardines have neither hair nor fur nor whiskers. Catfish have whiskers but catfish don't come in a sardine can, so there you are."

"Well, maybe so, but I could swear . . . "

"Swearing and cursing will never get you anywhere, Drover. You'd be much better off learning to control that temper of yours."

I returned to my dreamy state. It was so wonderful, I can hardly describe it. My body had become a battleground, as the Knights of

Warmth chased the wicked Demons of Cold down my spine, out to my legs and feet and . . .

My dreams were interrupted by Slim's voice. "Hank, for crying out loud, your hair's on fire!"

HUH?

G.L.Holmes

Someone was slapping me on the back, and all at once I smelled . . . well, burned hair, or something very close to it. And there was Slim . . . somehow my hair had . . .

"Hank, you do-do, get back from that stove before you burn my house down!"

My hair is very thick, you see, and sometimes it's hard to feel . . . I still say that sardines don't have . . . but just as a precaution, I moved away from the stove.

I turned to my assistant. "We'd best keep our distance from this stove, Drover. It's hotter than you might think."

"Did you catch on fire?"

"I wouldn't put it exactly that way, no."

"I knew there was something fishy going on."

"That was *sardines,* Drover, and I think we can drop the subject now. You were wrong but at least you tried. Next time, try a little harder."

"Oh. Okay."

That took care of that.

Yes, I know. We haven't gotten to the business about the ghosts yet, but it will come. In this old life, one thing must follow another, just as one thing must precede another.

It seems to work better that way.

CHAPTER

2

THE MYSTERY OF THE TALKING PETUNIA

Slim had nibbled off half his sandwich, and now he stuffed the other half into his mouth, filled her plumb up until his cheeks puffed out. He paced the floor in front of us, chewing his supper and wiping his hands on his jeans.

"Poborrow wul huff to cwee iss house up."

Drover and I stared at him, and twisted our heads at the same time.

He chewed some more and swallered a lump of sandwich that was so big, it made his eyes bulge.

"Tomorrow, we'll have to clean this house up. My petunia's coming over for Halloween supper, and I'd hate for her to think I live like this all the time." He ran a toothpick around

13

his teeth and scowled. "I don't understand how this place gets in such a mess. I cleaned it up . . . July, I guess it was."

He shook his head, went back into the kitchen, and had a Twinkie for dessert.

Drover turned to me. "What's a petunia?"

"A petunia is a variety of flower."

"He's having a *flower* over for supper?"

"That's correct."

"I'll be derned. What would you feed a flower?"

"Water and flower food, I suppose."

"What would you talk about with a flower?"

"You'd talk about . . . you heard what he said. He's having a flower over for supper and he wants to clean up the house because he doesn't want the flower to think he's a slob."

"I didn't know flowers could think."

I glared at the runt. "Flowers *don't* think, and they don't talk either. That's part of their charm. You might try it yourself sometime."

"But I thought you said . . . "

"Never mind what I said. It's what I *meant* that matters. Now stop asking meaningless questions."

"Oh. You mean . . ."

"Exactly. Dry up."

14

He dried up for a whole fifteen seconds. Then, "How do you reckon a petunia chews its . . . "

"Drover!"

" . . . food?"

"Shhhh!"

At last, silence. I curled up beside the fire and prepared myself for a nice, long, warm sleep in front of the stove. Not only did I not know how a petunia chewed its food, but I didn't care.

That was Slim's problem. If he wanted to socialize with flowers . . . I just didn't give a rip, is what I'm saying.

I had just drifted off into a wonderful twitching dream about my one and only True Love, the fair and lovely Miss Beulah, when I heard . . . singing? Singing in the distance?

I raised my head and glanced at Drover, who was curled up in a white furry ball and appeared to be fast asleep.

"Was that you?"

His head came up and one eye fell open. "Murgle skiffer."

"I said, was that you?"

"When?"

"Just a second ago."

"Well, I don't know if it was me or not.

15

What did I look like?"

"No, you don't understand. I thought I heard . . . listen!" We cocked our ears and listened. There it was again!

Oh brethern ain't you happy?
Oh brethern ain't you happy?
Oh brethern ain't you happy?
Ye Followers of the Lamb.

Yes, it was singing, and it appeared to be coming from outside the house.

Suddenly the hair on my bris backled up . . . the hair on my back bristled up, I should say, and a growl came from deep inside my throat. I sprang to the north window, sniffed the curtains, and . . . sneezed. They were very dusty, don't you see, but after sneezing twice, I barked.

Slim came out of the bathroom, wearing a nightshirt that exposed his bony knees and skinny legs. He came over to the window, walking on crumpled-up toes because the floor was so cold.

"What is it, Hank?"

I barked again. *Someone or something was out there in the night, prowling around and singing without permission.*

16

Slim narrowed his eyes and tugged on his chin whiskers and listened. "I don't hear anything."

He didn't hear . . . well, fellers, I could hear it, plain as day! I hopped my front legs up on the window sill and barked louder than ever. I mean, this was getting serious. We had trespassers out there in the night, and you know where I stand on the issue of trespassing.

I don't allow it, never have.

I was all set to dive through the window, ready to by George take out glass and screen, the window frame, even part of the wall if necessary. I mean, I was that stirred up. But Slim called me off.

He started down the long, dark hall that led to the back bedroom. "Come on, dogs, I've got a job for you."

Drover went streaking down the hall, and I followed.

Funny thing about that house. The farther away from the stove we went, the colder it got. Slim's bedroom was about right for hanging meat. It was so cold back there, our breath made fog in the air.

Slim turned on the light. He was hugging his arms by this time and standing on the sides of his feet, and his teeth were chattering.

He pointed towards the bed—a bare mattress laid across squeaky springs and covered with two old quilts and a cow hide. He jerked the covers back and said, "Up! Come on, dogs, jump up!"

Okay, if that's what he . . . we jumped up and he pulled the covers over the top of us. All at once it was very dark and very COLD. Then we heard Slim's footsteps on the floor. It sounded as if they were heading back towards the living room.

I heard Drover's voice in the darkness. "Hank? I'm f-f-freezing! What are we doing under here?"

"I'm n-n-not sure at this point, but it probably has something to do with that noise we heard. Apparently Slim wants us to hide under here until s-s-s-something develops."

"I think I'm developing f-f-frostbite."

"I know what you m-mean, Drover. This may very well turn out to b-b-be the c-coldest bed I've experienced in my entire career."

"I think it's the c-coldest bed in the whole w-world."

My teeth were chattering so badly that I couldn't speak. For several minutes we lay there shivering in the darkness, waiting for someone to make the next move.

It was clear by this time that Slim had devised a clever trap for the trespassers. Yes, of course. It was an old trick, see. You hide your secret weapons, lure the villains into the house, and then, when they least expect it, you spring the trap on them.

Pretty smart.

We waited. My ears were perked, my entire body was poised for action. I heard footsteps coming down the hall. Someone was walking . . . no, someone was *running* towards the bedroom!

"Get ready, Drover, I think this is it."

"I'm so cold . . . "

"Shhhhh."

The footsteps came closer and closer. Now they were in the bedroom. Someone switched off the lights and then . . .

I hate being used. It gives me a lousy feeling deep inside the inner receptacles of my mind. It makes me . . .

Okay, here was the deal. Very simple. Slim put me and Drover into his cold bed so that we could warm it up for him. While we lay under the covers, shivering and fighting off frostbite,

he had gone back to the living room and warmed his backside on the stove.

That's why he had been so anxious for us to go home with him. It had nothing whatever to do with lonesomeness or trespassers. If I'd known that . . . oh well.

When he was sure we had pre-heated his bed, he came loping back into the room and jumped under the covers. Right off, I got a foot in the face. You know what he said?

"Get that cold nose away from me!"

Well, there was a very good reason why my nose . . .

It turned out to be a pretty rough night. Slim did everything in his sleep but sleep. He talked, he moaned, he thrashed, he snored, and most of all, he kicked. And then there was Drover's twitching and wheezing.

Noisiest bed I ever slept in.

Sometime in the middle of the night, I decided I'd had enough. I poked my head out of the covers and was about to go in search of a quieter place to sleep when all of a sudden . . .

I perked my ears and listened. There it was again, *that same eerie music coming from outside the house.*

Oh brethern ain't you happy?
Oh brethern ain't you happy?
Oh brethern ain't you happy?
Ye Followers of the Lamb.

Fellers, I didn't know who that was or why they were out there singing in the cold, but I never would have guessed that it might be *a bunch of ghosts.*

CHAPTER
3

SLIM CLEANS HOUSE

S lim was a single man, don't you know.
Sally May often referred to him as "a dirty
bachelor."

Exactly what "bachelor" meant, I wasn't
sure, but I understood the "dirty" part. His
house, for example. The next morning he
hopped out of bed and chunked up the stove.
Then he came streaking back and crawled under the covers again. While he waited for the
stove to warm up, he talked to me and Drover.
We had poked our heads out from under the
cow hide.

"Boys, I hate to take radical action, but if
Miss Viola was to see this place in the shape it's
in, she might think I live this way all the time."
I looked at Drover and he looked at me.

"Now, she don't like clutter so we've got to

move a few things around. And she don't like mice, so we'll have to do some whittling on the mouse population. Do you boys think we can handle it?''

I barked and tried to whap my tail under the covers. Slim had definitely picked the right dog for the mouse job. There wasn't a cat or dog in the county that could beat me at mousing, when I really put my mind to it.

Slim heaved a deep sigh. "Well, we ain't getting any younger or any better looking. I guess we'd better start cleaning the dadgum house.''

He pulled on his clothes and boots and we all went out and backed up to the stove. For half an hour or more Slim stood in front of the stove, making sour faces at all the junk in the living room and wondering where he ought to begin.

That was something to wonder about, all right. Shall I try to describe the house? Okay.

Living room: Four pairs of dirty socks, two undershirts, three towels, one pair of red longjohn underwear, one pair of jeans, three boots, two spurs, a pair of chaps, two saddle blankets, two catch ropes, one pigging string, and one old boot top that had been sewed at the bottom so's it would hold cow medicine.

That was only the top layer. Beneath all that stuff was a six-month supply of reading material: *The Livestock Weekly, The Cattleman Magazine, Western Horseman,* and the *Ochiltree County Herald.*

Coffee table: Three cups partially filled with coffee, and one of them had two dead june bugs floating around on the top; four empty pouches of Taylor's Pride chewing tobacco; a corncob pipe and a tin of Prince Albert's tobacco; an empty cracker box, an empty sardine can that had been used as an ash tray, and the wrappers from three Snickers candy bars; a bottle of three-way cattle vaccine, a dehorning tube, and a whet rock; cracker crumbs and pipe ashes, one banana peel and the core of an apple.

Hanging on the knob of the closet door was a pair of striped boxer shorts, and spilling out of the closet was a saddle, a pair of shotgun chaps, two more boots, a pair of five-buckle overshoes, and a sheeplined coat.

From my position in front of the stove, I couldn't see much of the kitchen, just a sink piled full of dirty pots and dishes, a skillet of cold grease on the stove, and a sack of garbage sitting beside the back door.

G.L. Holmes

Oh, and on the kitchen table: two empty jelly jars, a jar of peanut butter, half a sack of bread, and more crumbs and jelly spills than you could count in an average ranch day.

I've never been what you'd call a fussbudget, but even I could see that this place had gone to seed.

Well, the minutes passed, then an hour, and still old Slim stood there in front of the stove, shaking his head and talking under his breath. Then, at last, he bit his lip and set his eyes in a hard squint.

"I don't know what I'm going to do with all this junk, but dang it, I've got to do something. Come on, dogs, I'll move junk and you catch mice!"

And with that, old Slim left the stove and charged into the middle of the mess. He went through that living room like a mowing machine, and fellers, mice were going every which direction, looking for a new home.

In the first thirty minutes, me and Drover notched up three head apiece, and we only nailed the slow ones and the cripples. The rest of them got away.

Saddle, boots, leggings, blankets, and ropes went flying into the closet. When it got so full that it wouldn't hold anything else, Slim pushed on the door until he got 'er shut.

Then he opened up the stove and started pitching in all the newspapers and magazines —and one sock, by mistake. He watched the sock burn up and said, "Well, there's one I won't have to warsh."

Next, he got a feed sack and went around the house gathering up all his dirty clothes. When he was done, he scratched his head and wondered aloud what he ought to do with the sack. He ended up putting it in the back of his pickup.

Then he turned to the kitchen mess. He washed two plates, two cups, two glasses, two knives and forks, and set them on the counter to dry. Then he got a cardboard box out of the shop and starting filling it up with dirty dishes, pots, pans, and his coffee pot.

When he had it crammed full, he opened the oven door, poked the box inside, and shut the door again. He was proud of that. I could tell, 'cause he winked at me and grinned.

Well, it was afternoon by this time and old Slim had worked himself down to a nubbin. He collapsed into the big easy chair beside the stove—"Need to rest my bones for a minute," he said—and fell asleep.

So did we. I mean, all that cleanliness had just wore us out.

Next thing we knew, Slim's boots hit the floor and he jumped to his feet. "Holy smokes, it's five o'clock and we ain't done yet!"

He grabbed the broom and started sweeping. I watched from my place in front of the stove. First he went through the living room, and managed to stir up enough dust so that Drover's allergies started acting up on him. Even I had a little trouble breathing.

Then he made his bed and scrubbed the bathtub until it turned *white.* By George, that was a revelation to me. I'd always thought it was naturally grayish-black.

From there he went to scrubbing on the toilet bowl. I happened to be standing in the door during this part of the deal. He was on his knees in front of the pot, looking down into the water. His hair had fallen down over his forehead. He filled his cheeks with air and let it out real slow.

"Next time, I think we'll eat supper at *her* house. This pot work is for the birds."

By the time he'd finished with the pot, his face was showing the miles and the years. He reeled out his pocket watch and held it up in front of his face. "Jeeee-manee Christmas, I should have started this a week ago!"

He jumped up, tore off his shirt, washed under his arms, brushed his teeth, throwed some smell-good on his cheeks, and ran into the bedroom. He changed his jeans and polished his boots and trotted down the hall to the kitchen.

Drover and I had been watching from the door. When we saw him coming, we scrambled down the hall to keep from getting trampled.

"Out of the way, dogs, I'm runnin' late!"

He ran into the kitchen and started pulling things out of the ice box. He laid ten weenies into the cold grease in the iron skillet (he saved his grease, see, and that way he never had to wash the skillet) and put the skillet on the burner.

Then he took a hunk of cheese, cut the mold off the outside, sliced it up, and laid cheese strips on top of the weenies.

While the weenies sizzled in the pan, he poked at them with a fork and said, "This is one of my special recipes, boys. Cowboy Round Steak. Won't old Viola be proud of us?"

He opened a can of pork and beans and set it on a burner to warm. He seemed a little shocked when the paper label caught on fire and the beans boiled over on the stove.

When he got his bean fire under control, he stood in front of the open ice box, staring inside and tugging on his chin whiskers.

"She'll want a salad, I guess." He pulled out a brown lump of something and turned it over in his hand. Oh, it was a head of lettuce. He put it back. "Maybe bread would be good enough."

He slammed the ice box door and went over to the dinner table. He opened up a plastic sack with seven or eight pieces of bread in it, pulled them out a piece at a time, scraped the mold off with a spoon, and laid them on a saucer. He glanced around the kitchen and smiled. "Meat, beans, and bread. That ought to be enough for any human, don't you reckon?"

I barked. Sounded pretty good to me.

It was getting along towards dark by this time. Slim turned off the fire under his Cowboy Round Steak, grabbed his coat and hat, and yelled, "Come on, dogs, it's time to go pick up my petunia!"

We dashed to the door and jumped into the back of his pickup. And off we went down the creek road to pick up Miss Viola.

(I might point out here that Slim wasn't actually having a flower for supper, as you might have thought. No. Now and then he referred to his lady friend as his "petunia," don't you see. Just thought I ought to point that out).

4

MISS VIOLA AND HER DOGS

Miss Viola lived in an old two-story house, maybe two-three miles down the creek from Slim's place. You go east on the creek road, see, and then when it curves back to the south, that's her place off to the right.

She lived there with her folks and a couple of smart aleck dogs named Black and Jack. Black was the bigger of the two and he was . . . well, black, of course. Jack was smaller, kind of a yellow-brown mutt. Neither one of them showed much class or breeding.

First thing that happened when we pulled up in front of the house was that them two dogs came running out to meet us, barking their little heads off. When Slim stepped out, they sniffed his boots and followed him up to the porch. Then, when he went inside, they came loping back to the pickup and started giving me and Drover a hard time.

Black said, "I dare you to get out of that pickup."

And Jack said, "Yeah, me too. That makes it a double-dog dare!"

I heaved a sigh. "Well Drover, it appears that we've been challenged. We have no choice but to get out."

"Oh, I don't know. Seems to me . . ."

"Get out, Drover.

"Okay."

We jumped down and faced the mutts. They growled and raised their hair and backed up a few steps. Then Black said, "You're in big trouble now, fella."

And Jack said, "Yeah, and you're going to be sorry, and you'd better not take one more step or you'll *really* be sorry."

I grinned and took one more step. Behind me, Drover did the same. We waited to see what the mutts would do about it.

I knew they wouldn't do anything, see. I mean, I'd run into their kind before, and very seldom did they ever . . . so I was kind of surprised when Black stepped forward and barked in my face. "Drover, did you see that?"

G.L. Holmes

"No."

"He barked in my face. That means that we move into Combat Alert. Prepare yourself for some violence and bloodshed."

"Maybe it was an accident."

"Stay behind me and cover the rear. This situation is liable to get nasty before it gets any dirtier." I marched over to Black and we went nose-to-nose. At close range, he appeared to be bigger than I had thought. That didn't make any difference to me, of course, except that . . . well, he was a pretty big dog, is all I'm saying.

Real big dog.

Funny, he hadn't looked that big from a distance. And neither had Jack.

They were both big dogs.

"You uh . . . barked in my face."

"Yeah."

"I saw you, so don't try to deny it."

"I ain't denying it."

"You realize, of course, that I saw the whole thing."

"Yeah."

"If it was a mistake, well, we might consider a formal apology."

Black curled his lip and showed his teeth. "It wasn't no mistake. I did it, I'm glad I did it, and if I had it all to do over again, I'd do it all over again."

"I see. In that case, I have no choice but to turn this thing over to my assistant. Drover, tell him what happens now."

Drover squeaked and his eyes crossed. "Who, me?"

"Tell him about your karate. Drover's a black belt in dog-karate. The last time he got into a fight, he killed three dogs and a horse.''

"I did?"

"Go ahead, tell 'em the whole story. They might as well know what they're getting into. It was the biggest mess I ever saw. I mean, the place was just solid with blood and bones.''

Black and Jack traded glances. Then Black said, "I think you're bluffin'.''

"Yeah," said Jack, "and so do I.''

"Do you? All right, let's have a little demonstration. Drover, walk up to the front porch and show 'em how you break porch pillars in half with one kick.''

Drover gulped. "One kick?''

"That's right, just one. 'Course, you guys need to understand that the whole porch is liable to fall down. If that's okay . . .''

"Wait a minute," said Black. He wasn't grinning any more. "It ain't okay to knock the porch down. We might get in trouble with the folks.''

"That's your problem. If Drover shows his stuff, something's going to be destroyed. There's no way around it.''

They went into a huddle, and while they whispered, I threw a glance towards the house. Slim and the young lady had come out on the porch and were talking to Viola's parents. I sure wished they would hurry. This deal showed signs of getting out of hand.

I guess Drover was feeling insecure. "Hank, I hate to tell you this, I know you'll be disappointed, but I don't think I can do all those things you said. And I don't remember killing three dogs and a horse."

"Shhh. Of course you don't. Can't you see what I'm doing?"

"Yeah. You're fixing to get me killed."

"I'm running a bluff, stalling for time."

"Oh. Gee, that's what they said they thought you were doing. How can you run a bluff when everybody knows you're bluffing?"

"They're not sure, Drover. Can you see the indecision in their eyes?"

"I see murder in their eyes."

"No, that's indecision. Now listen. We've got a bluff going and we have to play it out. Just say your lines and try to look mean. And remember, as long as you're bluffing, nothing is real and no one'll get hurt."

"Just bluff, huh? Well, I guess I can try."

I glanced towards the porch again, and the next thing I knew, Drover had walked up to Blackie and whopped him across the nose.

G.L. Holmes

"There's for nuthin', mister. Now do something and see what happens."

Black and Jack stared at him—in disbelief, I would say, which was pretty muchly the way I stared at him too. Black starting growling and Jack started laughing.

"Yuk, yuk, yuk. He hit you on the nose!"

You know what Drover did then? He hit Jack on the nose! "What are you laughing at, smarty-pants?"

"Drover!"

He looked back at me and grinned. "Am I doing all right, Hank?"

Judging from the dark scowls on the faces of the two thugs he had just slapped, I calculated that the answer was no. They stood up, rolled their shoulders, and surrounded him.

Black spoke first. "You know what happened to the last dog that slapped me?"

"No, what happened to him?"

"He spent three weeks in the vet clinic."

"Oh," Drover grinned, "you're only bluffing, you can't fool me."

"Drover!" At last I caught his eye and shook my head. I had to let him know that those guys *weren't* bluffing.

It didn't work. The silly grin remained. At that moment, Black and Jack tuned up and started growling, and fellers, I'm talking about the real thing. They sounded like a couple of semi-trucks going up a long hill.

At last the awful truth began to penetrate Drover's tiny brain. His grin slipped a few notches. He turned his eyes on Black's big white teeth.

"Nuthin's real . . . when you're . . ." He looked at me. "Hank, are you sure they're bluffing?"

I gave my head a shake.

Drover gulped. "Oh my gosh. That means that I . . ."

I gave my head a nod. And right then, before my eyes, Drover fainted, the little . . . I could have wrung his . . .

Black and Jack lifted their eyes to me. Black flashed a wicked grin. "Karate, huh? Tears down porches, huh?"

"Well, uh, Drover has a heart condition, see, and sometimes . . ." They were moving towards me. "Now hold on, guys, I'm sure we can talk this . . . tell you what, if you'd like to . . . I think what we have here is a simple breakdown in . . ."

They jumped into the middle of me and the wreck was on. You know what? Those were two of the biggest dogs I'd ever seen in my entire life, and you talk about bite and scratch and kick! Holy smokes, they were in the process of taking me apart, piece by piece and leg by leg, when all at once Slim and Miss Viola came rushing out.

He grabbed Black and she grabbed Jack, and they pulled them off. Miss Viola was pretty well steamed up.

"Jackie, you naughty dog, what in the world do you think you're doing! And Blackie, you ought to be ashamed of yourself!"

It was then that she saw Mister Faint-When-You-Need-Him-Most lying in the middle of the driveway. She gave a cry and ran to him and gathered him up in her arms.

As though by magic, he let out a groan. "Oh, my leg!"

Miss Viola marched over to her two dogs. By this time they were sitting beside the yard gate with their heads hung low and their tails tapping the ground.

"You big bullies, see what you've done? Beating up Slim's poor little white dog, and they're here as our guests! I'm so embarrassed!"

Well, Miss Viola laid down some mighty stern messages to her dogs. Her folks had come down off the porch by this time, and they were shaking their heads and making apologies to Slim.

While they were busy with that, I decided this would be a good time for me to even the score and put the whole thing in its proper prospectus.

I walked over to the gate, lifted my leg, and blasted the gate post.

Pretty slick maneuver, if you ask me. See, Blackie and Jackie couldn't . . .

Only problem was that Slim eased around and booted me in the ribs. Didn't make any sense to me. I mean, I was making points for OUR side, right? Nevertheless, he booted me in the ribs—hurt too—and said, "Hank, get in the pickup!"

Well, to wrap this thing up, I loaded myself into the back of the pickup while Slim opened the door for Miss Viola. Mister Half-Stepper got to ride up front, of course, and Miss Viola fussed over him all the way back to Slim's place.

But the important point to remember in all this is that we— I, actually—had protected the reputation of our ranch and had scored points against a dangerous adversary.

Did Slim appreciate any of this? I'm not sure that he did, because as he was opening his door to get in, he looked back at me and said, "I ain't *ever* taking you on a date with me again, dog."

Makes you wonder, don't it?

CHAPTER
5

MISS VIOLA'S PECULIAR EATING HABITS

In our part of the world, when the sun goes down in November, it gets cold. And when you're riding in the back of the pickup, it's colder yet. By the time we made it back to Slim's place, I was near froze.

Now, I had a suspicion that Slim planned to leave me outside—not because I had done anything wrong, don't you see, but just because I had gotten myself involved in an incident with Miss Viola's hoodlum dogs, and I want to emphasize that *they had started the whole thing.*

The point is, I wanted to spend a quiet evening in front of the stove, so when Slim opened the front door for Miss Viola, I sort of slithered past her legs and made a dash for the stove, hoping that maybe Slim wouldn't . . .

"Hank, get out of here! We've got a lady in the house."

Miss Viola came inside, holding The Invalid in her arms. I established eye contact with her right away, gave her my most pitiful look, and whapped my tail against the hearth.

She had a good honest face, friendly eyes, and a nice smile. I had a feeling that she liked dogs and that we could do business together. I mean, here was a good old country gal who had growed up around dogs.

"Slim, it's not going to bother me if you let him stay inside. He can't be any worse than those two dogs of mine."

See? I had her pegged. Me and Miss Viola were going to get along just fine.

Slim chewed on his lip and frowned at me. "Well . . ."

"It's awfully cold outside. If I were a dog, I'd want to be in here by the stove."

"Well . . . all right." He came over to the stove and pointed a bony finger at my face. "You mess up one more time, and I'll pitch you out of here in a New York minute, you got that?"

Yes sir! No more messing up for me . . . even though I hadn't messed up the first time.

While Slim was busy with me, Miss Viola removed her coat and headed for the closet door. Old Slim's eyes got big and he went dancing across the room.

"Whoa now, Miss . . . you better not . . ."

Too late. She twisted the knob, the door flew open, and she came within an inch of getting buried under an avalanche of saddles, blankets, boots, and so forth.

She stared at all the stuff. Slim stared at it too. His face got a little red around the edges and he tried to smile.

"That's my junk closet."

"Oh."

"Let's put your coat on the chair."

He took her coat and then she took off her hat. It was a black hat with red things around the crown. They might have been grapes, cherries, wild plums, or small tomatoes.

Ordinarily I would have sniffed it out, because it seemed a little peculiar to me. Why would anyone decorate a perfectly good hat with vegetables? But under the terms of my probation, I didn't dare leave the stove. Wild horses couldn't have dragged me away from that stove.

So the Mystery of the Vegetables on the Hat

remained a mystery. All I could figger was that Miss Viola had brought some extra food, just in case what Slim fed her wasn't fit to eat.

Not a bad idea, actually.

Miss Viola brought The Invalid over to the hearth and set him down beside me. She rubbed him behind the ears and said, "There, I think you'll be all right." And then she went into the kitchen where Slim was putting the grub together.

I turned to Drover and gave him a withering glare. "I can't believe you did what you did."

"What did I do?"

"First off, you got those hoodlum dogs so stirred up they were ready to kill somebody."

"I was only bluffin'. That's what you said to do."

"And then, when you had 'em tuned up for murder and mayhem, you took the chicken's way out *and fainted.*"

"Well, I have these spells . . ."

"For that performance, Drover, you win the Chicken Award of the Month."

"Gosh, thanks, Hank."

"Don't thank me. It's no honor. It's a disgrace, and I must warn you that this will go into your dossier."

"Oh darn. But it sure was nice, riding home with Miss Viola. Makes a guy want to faint more often."

I stared at the runt. He had missed the point of my lecture. He had missed the point of every lecture in the entire world. Lectures were wasted on such a brick-head.

At that very moment, I heard a woman scream in the kitchen. Well, you know me. When it comes to protecting women and children, I get very serious, and before I could even think about it, I leaped up from the hearth and made a dash for the kitchen.

As you might have surmised, the scream came from Miss Viola, seeing as how she was the only . . . Miss Viola had screamed. That much was clear. What wasn't so clear, and what I had to determine right away, was what had caused her to scream.

Slim was standing over the stove, taking up the weenies with a fork. When he heard the scream, he dropped the fork and whirled around.

"Why Miss Viola, what's wrong?"

She held one hand up to her mouth, and her eyes were wide with fear. "Oh . . . I thought I saw . . . a mouse!"

Slim swallered, and that thing on his neck, adam's apple I guess you call it, jumped up and down. "A mouse? Why, that don't seem right. We've never . . . Hank, you stay in here and watch. We may have a mouse in here."

We may have a mouse in here?

Fellers, I'd spent a good part of the afternoon herding mice in that place, and I had reason to suspect that Slim wasn't telling . . . oh well. I just work here.

I sat down beside Miss Viola and concentrated on protecting her life from "a mouse," so to speak.

Old Slim had turned his back on the food, and by the time he got himself turned around again, everything on the stove was either boiling over or on fire. You never saw such smoke! Blue smoke, gray smoke, white smoke.

He shut off the burners and opened the back door and fanned the air with his hands. "Got a little smokey in here," he laughed.

I *think* he was the one who said it. It was hard to tell since we couldn't see the top half of his body.

I glanced up at Miss Viola. She had a kind of cement smile on her mouth, and she coughed into her hand.

Slim took up the weenies on a plate and put the plate in the middle of the table. While he was dumping the can of beans into a bowl, Miss Viola leaned over and studied the weenies.

They *did* look a little strange: something black and red and yeller, with smoke still curling up from them.

"What is *that*?" asked Miss Viola.

"That's Cowboy Round Steak, one of my best recipes."

"No, I mean *that*."

Slim's eyes followed her finger. He leaned over and stared at the plate.

"Is it . . . is it a roach?" she asked.

"Oh no. No, it's not a roach. Cricket, maybe." He picked it off the plate and pitched it out the door. "Must have hopped into my grease. I save my grease and sometimes . . . it's all right now. Let's eat." They sat down and bowed their heads, and Slim asked Miss Viola to say the blessing.

" . . . and Lord, help us through our times of testing, for Thou knowest that we're not as strong as we need to be. Help us to find order in chaos, help us to find the good in all things. Bless this . . ." She coughed. " . . . food to the nourishment of our bodies and we'll give Thee the praise. Amen."

"Amen!" said Slim, as he shook out his napkin and spread it across his lap. "Well, dig in, Miss Viola. We've got meat, beans, and bread. Who could want more?"

She smiled, and took small helpings of weenies and beans.

"Now, we've got plenty, so don't be bashful." Miss Viola had a little trouble cutting her weenie with the fork, so she sawed off a piece with her knife.

"Oh, Slim, did you do that drawing on the wall?"

Slim turned around and looked, and suddenly . . . HUH?

Say, this was very strange. All at once Miss Viola was holding a weenie in front of my nose. Well? I ate it, of course.

"No, no, that's my Ace Reid calendar. They give 'em out at the feed store."

"Of course. I see now."

"Say, you're out of round steak. Have some more."

He rolled another weenie onto her plate. She thanked him and sawed off a chunk.

"But Slim, isn't that calendar out of date?"

He turned around again and . . . another weenie in front of my nose?

"By gollies, you're right," said Slim. "These years come and go, don't they? It's kind of hard for a guy to keep up."

I ate the weenie. Sure had a load of garlic in it.

No sooner had I swallered the weenie than there was a piece of bread in front of my nose. Well heck, I wolfed it down, and Miss Viola gave me a good petting behind the ears.

Slim glared at me, then set his knife and fork down on the table. "Hank, I think it's time for you dogs to go outside. How can a poor lady enjoy her supper with you hanging around and begging for food? Come on, Drover, you too."

Little Drover came padding around the corner. He was wearing his usual simple grin and blinking the sleep out of his eyes.

Slim opened the back door and pointed out into the darkness. As I was leaving, I glanced back at Miss Viola. Unless my eyes played tricks on me, I saw her wrap up the rest of her weenie in a napkin and slip it into her purse.

She was a mighty nice lady, but she sure had some strange eating habits. Very strange.

CHAPTER
6

STRANGE AND EERIE
SOUNDS IN THE NIGHT

The door slammed behind us and we found ourselves outside in the darkness and the cold.

Drover began shivering and moaning and looking up at the cloudy sky. "Hank, I sure wish we could have stayed inside, don't you? It seems awful spooky out here."

"All good things come to an end, Drover, and as for the spookiness of the situation . . ."

It *was* kind of spooky, to tell you the truth. For one thing, I didn't know my way around Slim's place. I had never spent much time down there, don't you see, and I wasn't too familiar with the way it was laid out.

For another thing, the wind was moaning in

the tops of the trees. I never did care much for a moaning wind. It gives me the jitters.

And then another thing. I remembered the singing I'd heard the night before. Now, I was something of a singer myself and had been known to belt out a few songs after dark, but let me tell you something. When I hear music in the night, I like to know where it's coming from. If it comes from nowhere, I get suspicious.

Also a little nervous.

Scared.

Don't get me wrong. I wasn't the kind of dog who believed in ghosts and goblins and such things, but . . . it was a spooky night.

"Don't let it bother you, Drover. This is just another night, one of many this old world has . . . what was that?"

"What?"

"I thought I heard something, a banging sound. Did you make a banging sound?"

He rolled his eyes around. "I don't think so, unless it was my heart. It's kind of banging around."

"No, this was something else." We listened, and there it was again: a banging sound. "Drover, I think we'd better check this thing out. Something strange is going on around here."

"Maybe it would be better if we stayed on the porch."

"No, that's a bad idea. Do you want to know why?"

"Not really."

"If we stayed on the porch, Drover, we'd be running away from our fears. We'd never learn what it was that caused us to be afraid."

"Yeah, that's what I like about it."

"Where's your curiosity? Your sense of adventure? Don't you want to plumb the mysteries of the Great Unknown?"

"I never was much of a plumber."

"Very well, if you insist on being a scaredy-cat and a chicken-liver, I'll go by myself. I'll take all the chances and then I'll take all the credit, while you go to the porch and hide from every little sound in the night. Is that what you want, Drover? Is that the way you want to conduct your life? You're old enough now to make your own decisions. The choice is yours."

"I think I'll go to the porch."

"Oh no you won't. You're going with me."

"But I thought . . ."

"The choice is yours unless you make the wrong choice. I can't allow you to make dumb decisions. Come on, let's move out."

We went creeping through the darkness, toward the sound of whatever it was that was banging. It was pretty tense there for a while, but the mission turned out to be a big success. We discovered that the door on the cake house had come unlatched, and it was banging in the wind.

"There, you see? It was nothing to be afraid of. But if I had let you go to the porch, you'd still be up there shivering and imagining all kinds of crazy . . ."

Suddenly I heard something else, a new sound. It was coming from a grove of bodark trees a short distance away. "Drover, did you hear voices? Unless I'm seriously mistaken, someone is lurking over in those trees."

"Hank, is this Halloween night?"

"No. We don't observe Halloween."

"Am I old enough to make a decision yet?"

"I suppose we can talk about it. How old are you now, Drover?"

"Well . . . I'm not sure. That depends on when I was born."

"That's correct. And when were you born?"

"That's the part I'm not too sure about. I think I was there but I don't remember much about it."

"You *think* you were there but you don't remember much about it. Is that what you're saying?"

"Yeah, my early years are kind of hazy."

"Were there any witnesses to this alleged event?"

"Well, let's see. My brothers and sisters were there, and so was my ma."

"None of whom is available to testify in your behalf, is that correct?"

"I guess so."

"In other words, we have no proof whatsoever that you were born. We still have no date of birth, and hence, no age. I'd say your case looks pretty weak, Drover."

"Can you remember when you were born?"

"Uh . . . why do you ask?"

"Well, if you can't remember when you were born, then how do we know you're old enough to make a decision about whether I'm old enough to make a decision?"

"Drover, the answer to that is so obvious that I won't even bother to say it."

"It is?"

"Yes."

"Well . . . what is it?"

"You really don't know? Do I have to spell it out for you?"

"No, just say it."

"Very well, I'll say it one time and I'll expect you to remember it."

"Okay, I'm ready."

"The answer is: *Shut up*."

"Oh."

"And quit asking moronic questions in the middle of an important investigation."

"What's a 'moronic question'?"

"The question you just asked is an example of a moronic question, and I forbid you to ask any more."

"How can I find out what 'moronic' means?"

"You can't. Now, I think we've settled the matter about your authority to make decisions, and once again you've proved yourself unfit and irresponsible. I'm sorry, Drover, but I have no choice but to make the decisions for both of us."

"How can you make a decision if you've got no choice?"

"Exactly. And always remember, Drover: I'm doing this for your own good."

"Does that mean we can't go home?"

"That's correct."

"Could we go back to the porch?"

"No. Any more questions before we launch our investigation of the mysterious voices in the trees?"

"I'm scared."

"That's not a question."

"Yeah, but it's true, and I want to go home!"

"The truth, Drover, is that you were born scared."

"I still don't remember a thing about it."

"And you'll just have to learn to live with it. All right, let's move out. We've got a job to do."

And with that, we went creeping into the darkness, towards the grove of trees from whence the mysterious voices had come. To find out what it was, you'll have to turn the page.

CHAPTER
7

TWO UGLY BLACK
THINGS IN THE TREES

I've already said that it was a spooky night, with the darkness and the wind and the moon half-covered with clouds. But the closer we got to that grove of bodark trees, the spookier the night became.

I can reveal here that entering dark groves of trees on dark spooky nights has never been something I've enjoyed doing. And that goes double when I can hear voices coming from the dark grove of trees.

And fellers, I could hear voices—whispering, mumbling, grumbling, rumbling voices.

The only thing that kept me going was iron discipline and Drover. Not that he provided me with any help or encouragement, understand. Far from it. But I knew that if I showed any outward signs of fear, it would ruin him.

I had to be a good example. That's part of my job.

Well, we entered the dark mysterious grove. The wind moaned and whistled through the trees, and their frozen branches made a terrible creaking sound.

Then, suddenly, one of the voices rose to a high pitch and I heard someone shriek, "Son, if you don't know where we're at, then what are we a-doing here?"

HUH?

I stopped in my tracks, and Drover ran into me, gave both of us quite a scare.

"Hank, did you hear that? I heard a voice!"

"Of course you heard a voice. That's what we've come to investigate."

"Yeah, but . . . I think it's a ghost!"

"A ghost? Don't be absurd. A ghost is nothing but a frigment of the imagination. That voice sounded familiar to me, and unless I miss my guess, we've cornered ourselves a couple of stray birds."

"Birds?"

"That's correct. Buzzards, to be exact. What they're doing in a place like this, I don't know, but we're fixing to find out. Come on, Drover, follow me and let me do the talking."

"That's fine with me. I've got nothing to say to a buzzard."

"Hush!"

I crept forward in the darkness, every muscle in my highly conditioned body tensed and ready for action. At the same time, my data banks were spewing out calculations on distance, lassitude, longitude, height, depth, speed, azimuth, apostrophe, and temperature.

To give you an idea of how these things work, here are some of the numbers I was receiving from Data Control: 3, 17, 29, 2, 94, 354, 49, 1, .0003, 3.56, and 1-800-555-1212.

Pretty impressive, huh? Those were real numbers, every single one of them, and I don't need to mention that no ordinary dog could have produced so many real numbers in such a short span of time.

As you can see from the read-out, we were getting close to the buzzards, so I shifted into the Stealthy Crouch Mode—stiffened my tail, extended my neck, raised my ears two notches, and switched the Raised Hackles circuit over from manual to automatic.

In other words, I was ready to engage the

Enemy. Those buzzards were about to get the surprise of their . . .

I'm not sure how it happened that I ran into them. We're still working a few little bugs out of the system, now and then we get faulty numbers, you have to remember that it was very dark. And that buzzards are black.

I ran into them, is basically what happened, and I'll admit that it came as something of a shock. An even greater shock followed when one of them began to squawk and flap his wings.

I think it was Junior. Yes, of course it was. Junior has a very distinctive way of speaking, and it would be hard to mistake him for anyone else, even on a dark night.

"W-w-w-wolf, w-w-wolf! H-help, me-me-me-me-murder!"

"Junior, you hush up, quit hollering about wolfs and figger out how we're gonna git outa this mess of trees, I never should have let you talk me into, son, if you cain't fly to wherever it is you're a-going, you shouldn't ort to go, is the way it looks to me!"

"B-b-but P-p-pa, there's a w-w-w-w-w-w-w . . ."

"There's a lesson to be learned, is what

there is, and the lesson is that a buzzard has no business . . ." There was a moment of dead silence. Then, "Son, what is that thang I see? It's hairy and it has a nose. Is it you?"

"N-n-n-n-no, it's n-not m-m-me, not me."

"In that case, what do you reckon it might be?"

"I th-think it's a w-w-w-w-wolf."

"A wolf?"

"Uh huh, a b-b-big w-w-w-w-w-wolf."

"Son, you have fooled around and got us in sirrus trouble, I told you we had no business tramping around in a bunch of dadgum trees, and now we've, what are you gonna say to that wolf?"

Silence. "Uh hi th-there, M-m-mister W-w-w-w-wolf."

"How's it going, Junior," I said.

"Oh g-g-gosh, P-pa, it ain't a w-w-w-wolf at all, it's our d-d-d-doggie friend! Hi, D-d-d-doggie."

"Who? Said what? Doggie friend?"

"Y-y-yeah, the one that's s-s-such a g-g-good s-s-s-s-s-s-s-s-s-s-s-s-s-s-s-s-s-s-s-s . . ."

"Spit it out, son, time's a-wasting."

"Singer! The one that's s-s-such a g-good s-s-singer."

Wallace pushed his way forward and brought his beak right up to my nose. "You mean that hammerheaded ranch dog? Yes, it is, I see it is, the same no-count dog that has got you in so much trouble in the past, you keep away from my boy, Dog, and don't you be giving him any more crazy ideas about becoming a singer when he grows up, if he ever does!"

"B-b-b-but P-pa, I w-want to b-b-be a s-s-s-singer, singer."

"He wants to be a singer," I said. "What's so bad about that?"

"You hush, Dog, nobody in this family, a singer's life is no life for my boy!"

I had sort of stepped into the middle of a family squabble. Ordinarily I don't do that, but Wallace had a way of getting on my nerves.

"Just because he sings doesn't mean he can't do the other things that buzzards do. Come to think of it, what do buzzards do?"

"We work the ditches and the highways to find our next meal, because, Puppy Dog, nobody feeds a hungry buzzard. We git no handouts and no free meals in this business, and we never will because we have our pride and our dignity."

"A buzzard has pride? What does a buzzard have to be proud of, if you don't mind me asking?"

Wallace stood up straight, tried to suck in his pot belly, and held his head high—as high as he could with a crooked neck.

"We're proud of our buzzardhood, is what we're proud of, and proud of our glorious history. We're proud of cleaning up the highways, and we're proud that no self-respecting buzzard has ever taken a free handout from nobody. And most of all, we're proud to be proud!"

"Y-y-yeah, w-we're sure p-p-proud, and h-h-hungry t-too."

"Yes, we are, we truly are, but just because we're poor and hungry and down on our luck don't mean that . . . say, neighbor, I don't suppose you have any food on you, just a little scrap of something to git us by until our luck changes, like maybe a piece of dead rabbit or a tough old rooster that nobody wants?"

"Nope. We're fresh out of dead rabbits and old roosters."

"So there you are, Junior, that's the kind of friend you have, selfish and stingy and don't give a rip for nobody but himself!"

"Y-y-yeah, but h-h-he can sure s-s-s-s-s-sing."

"Son, the world is full of singers. What we need around here is a good honest meal. Anybody can sing."

"Y-y-you c-c-can't." Wallace glared at Junior and Junior grinned at me. "I g-g-got him there, 'cause h-h-h-he c-c-can't s-s-s-s-s-sing, can't sing."

"I can too sing!"

"C-c-can't."

"Can!"

"C-c-c-can't."

"Can too! And what's more, I'll prove it. Yall just stand back and give me some room and I'll show you a thang or two!"

I wouldn't have bet a nickle that the old buzzard could have carried a tune, but you know what? We moved back and gave him some room, and he tuned up his tonsils and spread his wings and sang a song called "Buzzard Love."

Buzzard Love

When I was a young bird, a sly golden-
   tongued bird,
The handsomest buzzard you ever did
   see,
The ladies all lined up and fought 'til
   they signed up
To kiss me each day at the base of my
   tree.

This one gal named Monique, she said
   that my technique
Was crude and stuck-up and completely
   uncouth.
She thought I was tryin' to impress 'em
   by lyin'
But shucks, I was trying to tell 'em the
   truth!

Oh Buzzard Love, on the wings of a
   dove,
You've left me here behind.
When I took up wimmen, 'twas like I
   was swimmin',
You throwed me a sinker instead of a
   line.

One night on our roost I reached out
and goosed
The ugliest daughter of a feller named
Roy.
Her name was Sue Ellen, she went
around smellin'
Of wonderful fragrances buzzards enjoy.

I figgered she'd squeal but it came as a
real
Surprise when she called me a miserable
creep.
To add to the drama, it seems that her
momma
Had moved in between us while I was
asleep.

Oh Buzzard Love, on the wings of a
dove,
You've left me here behind.
When I took up wimmen, 'twas like I
was swimmin',
You throwed me a sinker instead of a
line.

I think there's a lesson for birds who go
messin'

With dynamite, gasoline, H-bombs, or
 gals.
Before you start kissin' on that
 nitroglycerin
Take out some insurance, get help from
 your pals.

Now, I'm here to witness, you'll need
 lots of fitness
As well as some help from the Lord up
 above.
'Cause birds of a feather can stir up bad
 weather.
A stormy condition they call Buzzard
 Love.

Oh Buzzard Love, on the wings of a
 dove,
You've flown away from here.
And now when I look up and wish I
 was hooked up
You drop me a whitewash instead of a
 tear.

8

JUNIOR CLAIMS HE SAW A GHOST

Well, Wallace finished his singing (or whatever it was) and looked pretty proud of himself.

"You said I couldn't sing, son. What do you have to say now?"

"Oh g-g-gosh, that w-w-was p-pretty g-g-g-good!"

"*Pretty* good? I'd say it was much better than that. I'd say it was very close to a work of art, myself."

"It w-w-was a w-w-work of a-a-art, P-pa."

"There, you see? We've hit the same conclusion, and you're right, son, it was truly wonderful, yes it was."

"It was w-w-w-wonderful, P-pa."

"Well, you ain't lost all your marbles, and as

long as you can still appreciate them old-timey songs, the trouble with these kids today is that they sing all this modern stuff and forgit that nobody has written a decent song since Bob Wills.''

"Y-y-yeah, I g-g-guess s-s-so."

"Did you realize that Bob come from Buzzard, Texas?"

"Uh, uh, I think it w-w-was T-t-t-turkey, T-texas."

"Turkey Buzzard, Texas, yes it truly was."

"Oh. M-m-maybe s-s-so."

"And I can't stand that noisy so-called music with the loud git-tars and the screamin' wimmen."

"Y-y-yeah, m-me too."

"Never could handle a screamin' woman."

"M-m-me n-n-neither."

"Because, you see, son, a song like 'Buzzard Love' has real feeling. It was written back when buzzards was buzzards, and wimmen was wimmen, and love was love."

"Y-y-yeah."

"And it teaches an important lesson about life, and son, no matter how you slice it or what kind of bottle you put it in, life is still life."

"Y-y-yeah, I g-guess s-s-so."

"And it's got nuthin' to do with screamin' wimmen or loud git-tars."

"Y-y-yeah, and I'd s-s-sure like to b-b-be a s-s-singer, P- pa."

"Well let me tell you something, son. Here tonight, in this very place, I've seen a change come over you. I've seen that good music has touched your heart. I've seen an uplifting of your taste in music. With these very eyes of mine, I've seen thangs I never hoped to see."

"Y-y-yeah."

"And son, on this very spot on this very night, I can foresee the day when you become a great and famous sanger!"

"Oh b-b-b-boy!"

"Yes you will, and I'll sang with you."

"Oh."

"And I can foresee the day, Junior, when me and you go from town to town and from hall to hall, through the highways and the hedges, singing together the only good song left in this terrible old world: 'Buzzard Love.' "

"J-j-just one s-s-song?"

"Yes we will, we surely will. And son, the crowds will come, and the people will come, and everyone will come from miles around to hear . . ."

I'd heard about all of Wallace's noise I could

stand. It was time for him to shut up. I had sat quietly through all that mess, and now I let out a big old loud snore.

"SKAWWWWWWWWW."

His head snapped around and he gave me an evil glare. "Just what do you think you're a-doin', Dog, you've interrupted my, if you can't stay awake, then maybe you ort to be taking worm pills!"

I pushed myself up. "I've got three things to say to you, Buzzard. Number One, nobody but a brick could listen to you very long without falling asleep."

"That's *one,* Dog, and you're already in trouble."

"Number Two, your taste in music comes real close to your taste in food. That was the worst song I ever heard, and if you just had enough time, you could put music completely out of business."

All at once, Junior's eyes lit up like headlights, and a big grin spread across his beak. "G-g-gosh, that's a t-t-t-terrible thing to s-s-say, hee-hee, hee-hee."

The old man's head snapped around to Junior. "If it's such a terrible thang to say, son, then how come it is that you have such a big smart-mouth grin on your face, you git that grin off your beak this very, and as for you, Dog, that's *two* and you're in even deeper trouble now."

"Number Three, you birds are trespassing on this ranch, making noise and creating a public nuisance, and it's my job to find out what you're doing here. It's strictly routine, of course, unless I uncover something suspicious."

Wallace puffed himself up. "We're here because we got lost, is why we're here, and we'll stay here until we figger out where we are, and you've got nuthin' to say about it."

"Y-y-yeah, w-w-we got l-lost 'cause w-we s-s-saw something s-s-scary, scary."

"Hold it, halt, stop right there, freeze!" I pushed myself up to the full alert position. "You say you saw something scary on this ranch?"

"Y-y-yeah, it was a g-g-g-ghost."

"Yes we did, we truly did," said Wallace. "It was the ghost of an old man, and he come right out of that cake house yonder, and he throwed such a terrible scare into us, we got off course and crashed into these trees here, is what happened."

I paced back and forth in front of them, studying their faces and sifting clues. "Okay, there's only one problem with your testimony. I don't believe a word of it, because I don't believe in ghosts.''

"Well, you just believe anything you want to, Dog, 'cause what we seen was a *ghost*."
"Y-y-yeah, and this is H-h-halloweeen n-n-n-night too!''

"Halloween means nothing to me. We've got no time for such foolishness.''

"H-h-halloween's the n-n-night when all the g-g-g-g-g-g, uh spooks c-c-come out.''

"Yes, and we seen one this very night with our own eyes, is how it happened that we got lost.''

"I see. Would you care to hear my analysis of your testimony?''

Old man Wallace narrowed his eyes and stuck his beak up in my face. "Pooch, after all the tacky and hateful thangs you said about my sanging, you have lost all credibility, and no, we wouldn't care to hear anything you have to say.''

"Well, that's tough. You'll hear my analysis, whether you like it or not.''

Wallace pulled his neck back into his shoulders and covered his ears with his wings. "I ain't going to listen, and Junior, don't you listen either, we've got our rights, we don't have to listen to no smart aleck ranch dog."

"In the first place," I said, "I don't buy your story about seeing a ghost. What you saw was swamp gas."

"Who's got gas?"

"N-n-no, h-he said s-s-swamp gas, P-pa."

"Well, if he's got gas, tell him to quit eatin' so much, it ain't our fault if he makes a pig of himself."

"In the second place, we don't believe in Halloween on this ranch, so as far as you're concerned, Halloween night has been called off."

"He hauled off what? What's he talkin' about, son?"

"H-h-he said H-h-halloween's b-been c-c-c-c-cancelled."

"What does he mean *penciled?* I can't understand what he's talking about."

Junior pried one of Wallace's wings away from his ear and yelled, "C-c-c-c-c-c-cancelled!"

"Son, you just spit in my ear!"

I went on with my analysis. "In the third place, you're trespassing on my ranch, and I think it's time you moved along and found another place to loaf."

"Another piece of rope? Who's got a piece

of rope? What's he talkin' about, Junior?"

"H-h-h-he s-s-s-said we have to l-l-leave."

Wallace dropped his wings and glared up at me. "Oh he did, did he? Well, that's fine with me, I didn't like these dadgum trees in the first place, you just tell us which way is north and we'll be more than happy to go find better company, which won't be hard to do."

"Fine," I said, "and that will make us all happy. From this point on the ranch, north is directly across from south, to the right of east and to the left of west. Now move along before I have to go to sterner measures."

"Never mind north and south, Dog, which way is *out*?"

"Follow me."

I made my way through the trees and led them out into the clear. It was at that point that I noticed Drover had vanished—deliberately disobeyed my orders and gone to the porch. Well, I would settle with him later.

I pointed up to the stars. "There's the sky, Buzzard, and here's the ground. If you intend to fly, point yourself up. If you're walking, stay on the ground. I can't make it any simpler than that. If you get lost again, ask a ghost for directions."

"W-w-we r-r-really did s-s-see a g-g-g-ghost, D-doggie."

"Of course you did, and I saw a flying codfish yesterday afternoon."

G. L. Holmes

"You'll be sorry, Dog, making fun of a couple of poor old buzzards who are down on their luck. Come on, son, let's git out of here before that ghost comes back and makes this dog pay for his evil deeds."

Wallace spread his wings and made a run into the wind. He got airborne, but took a couple of shingles off the roof of the chickenhouse.

Junior gave me a grin. "W-w-well, goodbye, D-d-d-doggie. P-pa don't s-s-sing so g-g-good, does he?"

I placed a paw on his shoulder. "You've got a lot to overcome, Junior. All I can tell you is . . . good luck."

And with that, Junior went running and flapping down the road, until at last he disappeared into the night sky.

Well, I had cleared up that little matter and was on my way to the cake house to check it out, when all of a sudden I heard someone running in my direction.

Expecting an attack by coyotes or monsters, I whirled around and let out a blood-chilling growl.

CHAPTER

9

THE CASE OF
THE MYSTERIOUS
TRICKER TREES

It turned out to be Mister Hide-on-the-Porch. I should have known.

"Hank, oh my gosh, come quick, help, murder, mayday, mayday!" Since the little mutt seemed to be almost beside himself, I decided to postpone bringing charges against him for cowardly and chicken-hearted behavior.

"All right, Drover, take it from the beginning and give me a full report. Try to control yourself and give me the facts."

"Well, I'll try, but I sure am scared."

"I can see that, but unless you can prove that you saw something scary, you're in trouble for leaving an investigation without permission."

"Yeah, but I DID see something scary! It scared me clean out of my wits."

"That proves nothing, Drover, because you have very few wits out of which to be scared."

"Oh. Okay."

"Nevertheless, I'll listen to your report. From the beginning, and hurry up. We have a night patrol to make."

Drover rolled his eyes. "Well, I was lying in front of the house . . ."

"Yes, on the porch, where you were told not to go."

"And a car pulled up in front of the yard gate, and the motor was running."

"Hold it right there. The yard gate doesn't *have* a motor, so it follows that the yard gate's motor couldn't possibly have been running. Already I've found a flaw in your story."

"No, I meant the *car's* motor was running."

"Oh. Well, I suppose . . . if you saw a car, Drover, and if the motor's car was running, as you claimed, then where did this alleged car go between the time you made your observation and the present moment?"

"It's right over there."

I turned my head and squinted into the darkness. There, parked in front of the yard gate, was a . . . well, a car. With its motor running, you might say.

"Hmm, yes, that checks out."

The car was black, see, and the night was also black, so it wasn't as obvious . . .

"All right, we have the car and the motor running. So far so good. Go on with your story."

"Well, I went over to the car . . ."

"Did you mark the tires?"

"No, not exactly."

"You should ALWAYS mark the tires of an unidentified vehicle, Drover. It's one of our most important jobs."

"I know, but I didn't have time, 'cause just then I saw . . ."

"Hold it right there. You *saw* something?"

"Sure did."

"Well, why don't you tell me what you saw?"

"I would, but you keep butting in."

"*Butting in*? Is that what you call it? Is that the thanks I get for trying to guide your testimony in the right direction? But never mind my feelings, never mind all the many things

I've done to help you. Go ahead and finish your story."

"I don't remember where I was."

"You had said something about a car."

"A car. A car? A car."

"That's correct, a car. The motor was running."

"Motor. Motor? Motor."

"Yes. The car had a motor and the motor was running."

"Are you sure I saw that?"

"Of course you saw it, and there it is over by the yard gate with the motor running."

"I thought you said gates don't have motors."

I went to sterner measures, showed him some fangs and gave him a growl. That got his attention.

"Okay, I think I've got it now. The car's gate was running over by the motor and I went to check it out, and that's when they got out."

I studied him in the moonlight. "Someone got out of the car? Did you give them a good barking?"

"No, I didn't have time. They were talking, Hank, real loud."

"Talking, huh? It's starting to come

together, Drover. I'm beginning to see a pattern here. Can you remember what they said?"

"Well, let's see. Something about trees."

"Trees? What kind of trees?"

"I don't remem . . . oh yeah. They yelled something about *Tricker Trees.* Then they went up to the porch and knocked on the door. Slim answered the door and they yelled, "Tricker Tree!" And everybody laughed and they went inside."

"Tricker Trees? Hmm. That seems odd. Why would someone come to the ranch at this time of night, leave the motor running in a car, go up to the porch, and talk about Tricker Trees?"

"I don't know. I never heard of a Tricker Tree before."

I ran my eyes across the darkness and tried to put this thing together. Something was missing.

"All right, Drover. Listen carefully and search your memory for every detail. You mentioned voices but you've said nothing about persons, places, or forms that might have produced these voices. Who were these people?"

"Oh my gosh, that was the scary part!"

I noted that he had begun to shiver. "Maybe you'd better tell me about it. I think we're getting to the heart of the core."

"Okay, I'll try, but I'm getting scareder and scareder. There were four of them, Hank."

"Yes? Four of them, go on."

"You won't believe it when I tell you."

"I'll be the judge of that. Go on."

"Well, all right. Oh Hank, there were four of them up there on the porch, yelling and screaming and shrieking about those Tricker Trees!"

"Yes, yes? Keep going. Who were they, Drover?"

"I can't say it!"

"Say it, spit it out!"

"You won't believe it!"

"Of course I will!"

"Two skeletons, one ghost, one witch, and a pirate!"

I glared at him. "I don't believe that, Drover."

"I knew you wouldn't, I never should have told you the truth!"

"Do you know why I don't believe it? In the first place, I don't believe in ghosts. In the second place, we don't have skeletons or witches on this ranch. In the third place, no pirate could survive in this country because our annual rainfall wouldn't support a pirate. They require large amounts of water."

"I don't care, I saw 'em with my own eyes."

"Let me finish. In the fourth place, you said you saw four figures on the porch. Two skeletons plus one ghost plus one pirate plus one witch equals *five,* Drover, not four."

"Maybe I miscounted."

"Maybe you miscounted or," suddenly I whirled around and faced him, "or maybe you're making all this up, Drover, creating a centrifuge to distract me from your insubordination."

"I don't even know what a centrifuge is. How could I create one?"

"Very easily. Let me explain. Do you know the meaning of life?"

"Well . . . not really. I'm still working on it."

"There you are. The fact that you don't know the meaning of life doesn't mean you're not living. Hence, by the same logic, the fact that you don't know the meaning of centrifuge doesn't mean you couldn't create one. Am I making myself clear?"

"I guess, but I still don't know what a centrifuge is."

"A centrifuge is a plot, a conspiracy, used by devious characters to cover up their devious behavior. It's one of the oldest tricks in the book, Drover, and you should have known better than to try it on me."

"I sure get into a mess when I try to tell the truth."

"Exactly. You made up the whole thing, and now that I've exposed your little fraud, what do you have to say for yourself?"

"I'm all confused."

"At last the truth comes out! You're all confused, Drover. What doesn't exist can't be seen, and I've already proven beyond a doubt that these so-called goblins couldn't possibly exist."

"I think I'll go back to bed."

"Not yet, Drover, not until we crack this case, for you see, we still have the mysterious black car with its motor running and we still haven't learned the identities of the Strangers In The Night."

"I don't want to know."

"Now let's get this case wrapped up. I will penetrate the yard and set up a forward position near the front steps."

"And I'll go to the machine shed and wait."

"I'm afraid not, Drover. The machine shed is two miles away at the other place."

"Oh drat."

"No, you'll serve as my backup and witness. We'll wait until they come out of the house. At that point you will see that they're only people, possibly the neighbors, and that will put a stop to these silly stories. Are you ready?"

"Hank, this leg of mine sure is giving me fits. Maybe . . ."

"Never mind the leg. We've got a job to do. Come on, son, over the fence and into the yard!"

And with that we leaped over the fence and set up our positions and waited for the trespassers to come out of the house.

CHAPTER

10

CAUTION: HAZARDOUS AND SCARY MATERIAL!

I sat down on the sidewalk, approximately ten feet in front of the porch, just beyond the halo of the porch light.

Behind me, I could hear the motor of the mysterious black car running. There was something about the car that bothered me. In fact, there was something about the entire case that bothered me.

On the surface, it appeared that The Case of the Mysterious Tricker Trees was moving along very well. I had suspects, a motive, and Drover's screwball conspiracy. But still . . .

Maybe there was something in the night air that made me uneasy. It was very dark, and off to the north I heard the moan of coyotes. Or maybe it was that business about the Tricker

Trees that bothered me.

That was the one piece of the puzzle that hadn't fallen into place. Why would strangers come to the ranch at that hour and ask for trees? And if they wanted trees, why had they gone into the house?

I had been in Slim's house that very day and I knew for a fact that he didn't keep trees in there. Mold, yes. Spiders, yes. Mice, yes. But no trees.

Off to my right I heard Drover's front paws scratching on the fence. The runt still hadn't made it into the yard.

"Hurry up and get over here. There's no reason why it should take you five minutes to climb over a fence."

"Well, I just can't seem to make it, Hank. I guess my legs aren't as strong as yours. Would it be all right if I stayed out here?"

"No, it wouldn't be all right, but if that's the best you can do, it's the best you can do. You're the one who has to live with yourself."

" Yeah, I wouldn't know where else to go."

Drover's yapping distracted me from my primary job, watching the front door. In other words, for a moment or two I lost concentration.

I didn't hear the front door open. I didn't

hear footsteps on the porch. I didn't know that I was about to be attacked until I turned around and saw . . .

I hesitate to describe what I saw. I mean, it was so horrible, so frightening, so blood-chilling that if I told the whole story, it might have a bad effect on the kids.

You know me. I worry about the kids. I don't mind giving 'em a little thrill now and then, but hey, when it comes to the real heavy-duty scary stuff . . . I don't know, it bothers me.

What I'm saying is that if there's any kids around who might have a bad reaction to heavy-duty hardcore scary stuff, you'd better take up their books right now before this thing gets wild.

Because it's fixing to get WILD.

Pause

Pause

Paws

Pa's

Pas (French)

You ready? Take a deep seat and grab hold of something solid. Here we go.

Okay. Let me set the scene again: dark night, coyotes howling off in the distance, a whisper of wind sighing through the bare limbs of the cottonwoods, and, behind me, the rumble of the motor of the Mysterious Black Car.

Just for a moment I had allowed Drover to distract me. Then I heard a sound to my left. It seemed to be coming from the porch. I turned my head and saw . . .

HUH?

Holy smokes, you won't believe this, hang on because here it comes . . .

TWO SKELETONS, ONE GHOST, ONE PIRATE, AND ONE WITCH!!!!

Fellers, I still didn't believe in skeletons or ghosts, but there they were right in front of me. Well, my ears flew up, just as though somebody had tied strings to them and give the strings a yank, I mean, we're talking about ears that almost flew off my head.

My eyes popped open, and I think they even crossed. My lower jaw dropped a good six inches and my tongue fell another six inches beyond that.

The hair on my back stood straight up, and I mean every single hair from my eyebrows all the way out to the tip of my tail, stood straight up, you'd have thought I was a porcupine.

Naturally, my first reaction to this nightmare was to bark, but when I tried to activate my barking mechanism, what I got was a squeak, not a bark.

Squeaking at goblins and skeletons is a poor response, but it was the best I could come up with on short notice. So I squeaked.

Up to this point I hadn't known whether these goblins were friendly or the dog-eating variety, but I soon found out. One of the skeletons saw me there, and at that very moment he or she (with skeletons it's hard to distinguish hes from shes) made claws with his or her hands, jumped at me, and screeched a poisonous magic word: "BUGABOOOOO!"

By then my feet and legs were moving. I could hear my claws scraping across the sidewalk, but they were moving at such an incredible high rate of speed that they couldn't get traction.

In other words, I was running in place, and I can reveal that my claws were throwing up sparks on the cement, and I mean showers of sparks that lit up the night.

You've seen guys welding after dark? Same deal: sparks, fire, smoke, the whole nine yards.

G. L. Holmes

Well, the first skeleton had laid a curse on me with that poisonous magic word, and that would have been serious enough in itself, but just then the other goblins came after me.

The second skeleton had a mysterious paper bag in his left hand. Gripping it at the top, he or she raised it above his or her head and began shaking it. It contained something, perhaps roots or magic herbs or even bones.

Yes, they were bones. See, when skeletons go walking around, sometimes their bones fall off and they carry a paper sack to hold all the loose ones. When they get back home, or wherever it is that skeletons go when they've finished terrorizing people and dogs, when they get back home, they have to stick all the loose bones back in place, otherwise they would soon fall apart.

So there you are, a little footnote on the behavior of skeletons.

And there I was, spinning my tires, so to speak, on the cement, and being attacked by two skeletons. Serious enough, right? Well, you ain't heard it all yet.

Suddenly this little witch jumped off the porch, and in case you haven't been attacked by any witches lately, let me describe this one. She was dressed in black, had a nose as long as a carrot, was missing two front teeth, and wore a very strange kind of pointed hat on her . . . well, on her head, of course.

In one hand she carried an object that resembled a broom. In fact it was a broom. Yes, I'm sure it was. In her other hand she carried a round orange object that resembled a punkin, but it was like no punkin I had ever seen before.

It was made of plastic, see, had a handle on it, and also a face. I know that sounds crazy, a punkin with a face, but this punkin by George had a face on it.

Anyway, this little witch . . . I say *little witch,* but come to think of it, maybe she wasn't so little. Maybe she was pretty big. In fact, she was HUGE.

This huge witch, she must have stood, oh, seven feet three inches tall, biggest woman I'd ever seen, she jumped off the porch and yelled, "Tricker Tree!"

And at that very same moment the ghost said, "WOOOOOO!" and he came flying off the porch.

Did I describe that ghost? Scariest thing I ever saw. No ears, no nose, no hair. Just two horrible eyes and a big round mouth. Oh yes, he was wearing tennis shoes.

And then the pirate came after me too. Description: little bitty short guy, must have been a midget or a widget or whatever you call those short guys, only this one was wearing a black patch over one eye, had two teeth missing and a big scar on the left side of his face, terrible scar with blood still showing, and he carried a sword.

Oh, and he was wearing tennis shoes too. That was another interesting clue, a ghost and a pirate wearing tennis shoes, but you might say that I wasn't in any position to put those two clues together and come up with a hypotenuse.

I mean, I was under attack, fellers. It was time to do some serious lifesaving.

One last thing about the pirate. When he jumped at me, he waved his sword and yelled those same two words: "Tricker Tree!"

Speaking of trees, it was time for this old dog to head for tall timber, but before I could get that deal accomplished, I had to endure one last shocker.

Slim and Miss Viola came to the door and looked out. Do you think they came to my rescue? Do you think they ran for a gun and started shooting? Do you think they even lifted their voices to help their loyal dog, their Head of Ranch Security?

No sir. Here's exactly what they did. Miss Viola slapped her knees, threw back her head, and *laughed*. That's right. She laughed!

And are you ready to hear what Slim did? He *roared* with laughter, and then he had the gall to yell, "Git 'em, Hankie, sic 'em, boy!"

Well, I had never been so . . . after years and years of loyal service . . .

Let's just say that this came as a bitter disappointment to me. It would have served them right if I had been eaten by those two skeletons. That would have left their dumb old ranch defenseless.

The time had come for me to, shall we say, fall back to another position. Or to put it another way, to run for my life.

At last my claws got traction on the sidewalk, and I went zooming away from this collection of goblins, spooks, and crazy people. No ordinary dog could have . . .

Only trouble was that I forgot to jump when I came to the fence, guess my mind was on other things, and boy did I come to a sudden stop, center-punched that dadgum fence and liked to have broke my nose off at the roots.

Well, I bounced off the fence, backed off and took another run at it and this time went flying over the top.

I don't know who parked the wheelbarrow over there, and don't particularly care, but it was a dumb place to park a wheelbarrow. I knocked it over, scrambled to my feet, and escaped a terrible death by a matter of inches.

It was then that I noticed that my legs were wet—very strange because I hadn't come in contact with any water whatsoever.

Beat anything I ever saw.

You may think the scary part is over, but just wait until you find out what happened in the cake house. Don't read the next chapter unless you're pretty derned tough.

CHAPTER

11

YOU'LL THINK IT WASN'T A GHOST, BUT IT WAS

Where do you go when you've got ghosts and goblins on your trail? I didn't know. I mean, they can walk through walls and see in the dark. It's hard to hide from that kind of enemy.

I went streaking away from the yard and came to the cake house, figgered that was as good a place as any, leaped through door and went inside.

It was very dark in there, with just a little rod of moonlight coming through the open door. I stumbled over junk and stuff, sacks of feed and wads of baling wire, and made my way back to the northwest corner, which was as far away from the door as I could get.

There, I found a stack of burlap feed sacks, and I proceeded to burrow under the sack on top. If those goblins wanted to eat me, they would have to eat a sack first.

And then I waited. I could hear my heart pounding: tah-DAH, tah-DAH, tah-DAH. I could hear the wind rumbling across the tin roof. And beyond that . . . nothing.

Nothing had ever sounded sweeter than the nothing I heard at that moment. I mean, I was ready for some heavy silence.

But then . . . what was that? Footsteps on the wood floor? Holy smokes, they were coming after me! I was backed into a corner and all I had for protection was an old cake sack.

My mind began racing, as I searched my data banks for some kind of response that would save me from those horrible creatures.

In this type of situation, did a guy come out fighting? Did he try to hide? What the heck did he do? It was kind of an important question, don't you see, because the wrong answer would get me more than a bad grade. It would get me . . .

I really didn't want to probe that matter too deeply. I wasn't sure what-all that collection of ghouls and goblins could do to an innocent dog, and I didn't want to know.

At last I came up with a plan. Instead of trying to hide or fight my way out, I would pretend that I was one of them—another ghost, in other words. It's common knowledge that one ghost won't eat another ghost.

Seemed reasonable that one ghost wouldn't eat another ghost.

I sure hoped that one ghost . . .

So I gathered my courage and raised up. I hoped that my legs wouldn't give out on me, because they were shaking.

And wet. I still didn't understand that part.

Disguising my voice, so that it sounded more like a ghost than a dog, I said, "Wooooo! Who's in my cake house?"

I heard the ghast gosp—the ghost gasp, that is. "Oh my gosh, who said that?"

"It's meeeeeee, the ghost of the cake house. You are disturbing my sleeeeeeep."

"Oh. Ohhhh. Ohhhhhhh!"

It was a ghost, all right. Yes sir, I had me a live one. The next question was, what could I do with him? Get rid of him, I think was my basic answer. But how?

Once again, I went into the Ghost Voice Mode. "What are you doing in my cake house?"

I heard a gulp, and then, "I'm hiding."

G. l. Holmes

"What are you hiding from?"

"From ghosts like you."

Hm. That was odd. A ghost who was hiding from another ghost? It occurred to me that this might be a ghost I could do business with. But first I would have to probe his thought patterns and develop a profile. It would require just the right touch.

"Tell me, spirit, why should you be hiding from a ghost?"

"Because I'm scared!"

"Why should a ghost be scared of another ghost?"

"I don't know, and I don't want to find out."

"Tell me, spirit, was it something that happened in your former life?"

There was a moment of silence. Then the ghost said, "I've never been a farmer."

"I said 'former,' not 'farmer.' "

"Ohhhhhhh."

This was getting me nowhere. Apparently this ghost didn't want to give out any information about his former life. Either that or he was a little stupid.

"Another question, spirit. Do you eat dogs?"

"I ate a hot dog once."

"But do you eat dogs?"

"No. Do you?"

Suddenly it occurred to me that I had heard that voice before. There was something about it . . . yes, I was almost sure I had. "Spirit, do you have a name?"

"Yes, but it isn't Spirit."

"I see. Well, we've eliminated that as a possibility, haven't we?"

"Yes."

"But instead of going through all the other

names in the language, maybe you could just come out and tell me what it is."

"Well, okay. If you promise not to eat me, I'll tell you that my name's Drover."

HUH?

Suddenly the pieces of the puddle . . . puzzle began to fall into place: The goblins had seized Little Drover, had killed him, and now he was a GHOST!

"Drover, listen to me. This is Hank."

"Hank!" I heard him gasp. "Oh my gosh, they got you, I knew you shouldn't have . . . Hank, I tried to help you, honest I did, but this leg . . ."

"I know you tried, Drover, but I just want to say right here and now that I regret all the mean things I've done to you."

"Yeah, and I regret all the chicken things I've done to you, and I hope you won't haunt me."

"Yes, well, that's exactly what I was going to say to you, Drover. I hope you won't . . . wait a minute. Did you say you hope I won't haunt *you*?"

"Yeah, please. I'll promise to be good for the rest of my life, and I'll take care of your ranch, honest I will."

Hmmmmmm.

"One last question, Drover. Are you a ghost?"

"Who me? A ghost? No, I don't think so."

"Well, I'm not a ghost either."

"Oh. Then . . . what are we doing?"

Ah ha!

I stood up and walked towards the sliver of light where Drover was standing. At last I had solved the case.

"What we're doing, Drover, is performing an exercise in futicity. I think I've finally got this thing worked out. This is Halloween night, Drover. Do you know what that means?"

"Yeah, 'cause Pete . . ."

"On Halloween, people who are ordinarily sane and normal dress up in masks and costumes, and go around trying to scare others."

"Pete told us . . ."

"Exactly. Those so-called goblins on the porch were just the neighbors' kids wearing costumes."

"Yeah, and Pete said . . ."

"Yes. You were duped. You gave me a false alarm and sent me into combat against a group of imposters. I had suspicions all along, of course, but I had to check it out."

"You mean . . ."

"Exactly. And another thing, Drover. You know the Tricker Trees you were telling me about? Those kids weren't saying 'Tricker Tree.' They were saying *Trick or Treat,* you little dunce, but you managed to garble the words just enough to throw me off the track. I should have known."

"What does Trick or Treat mean?"

"How should I know what it means? But that's what kids say on Halloween night. They always have and they always will, and it has nothing to do with trees."

"Oh, I'm so glad! Does this mean that we don't have to believe in ghosts any more?"

"That is precisely what it means, Drover. As I've told you many times, there is no such thing as a ghost. A ghost is nothing but a frigment . . . what are you looking at?"

He was staring with wide eyes toward the back of the cake house. "Hank, there's a man standing over there."

"Impossible. There was no man in here when we arrived and no one has come through that door. Hence, there can't possibly be a man standing back there."

"But I see him, and Hank, he looks like a ghost."

114

I couldn't help chuckling at that. "A ghost, Drover? Look again. Maybe he's a pirate. Or a skeleton, or maybe even a witch."

'No, he's a ghost, I just know he is."

"Drover, when will you ever learn? What does it take . . ."

He started backing toward the door. "Hank, I want to get out of here! That guy doesn't look natural to me."

"Drover, only a dope could be duped twice in one night. I've tried to explain . . ."

At that moment I heard voices. Someone was singing . . . the same mysterious . . .

I turned and looked towards the . . . HUH?

There stood an old man, wearing a long black coat. He was holding a hymn book in his hands. He was singing. He glowed in the dark. He looked very much like . . .

"Come to think of it, Drover, it seems a little stuffy in here, maybe we ought to step outside and get a breath of . . ."

We both edged toward the door, but at that very moment THE DOOR SLAMMED SHUT.

Uh oh.

We were trapped inside the cake house with a . . . fellers, I didn't want to jump to any hasty contortions, but that *thing* looked very much like a . . .

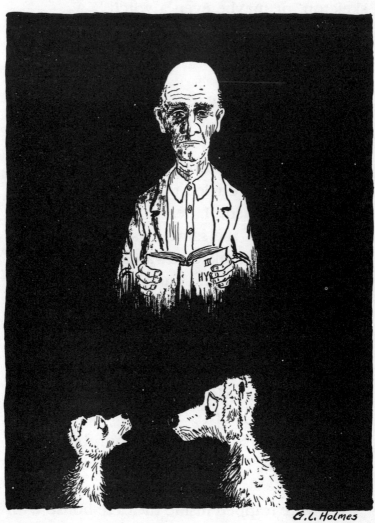

G.L. Holmes

GHOST!!

CHAPTER

12

DON'T WORRY, WE ESCAPED BUT JUST BARELY

In the darkness, we listened to the song. I mean, we didn't have a whole lot of choice.

It started out with just the old man singing, then a whole bunch of voices came in, until it was a whole entire chorus of voices singing. Here's how it went:

Followers Of The Lamb

Oh brethern ain't you happy?
Oh brethern ain't you happy?
Oh brethern ain't you happy?
Ye Followers of the Lamb.

Oh sisters ain't you happy?
Oh sisters ain't you happy?
Oh sisters ain't you happy?
Ye Followers of the Lamb.

Oh sing on, dance on, Followers of Emanuel!
Oh sing on, dance on, Followers of the Lamb!
Oh sing on, dance on,
Sing on, dance on!

I'm glad I am a Christian,
I'm glad I am a Christian
I'm glad I am a Christian,
Ye Followers of the Lamb!

Sing, dance!
Sing, dance!
Sing, dance!
Sing, dance!

Oh sing on, dance on,
Ye Followers of Emanuel,
Oh sing on, dance on . . .
Ye Followers of the Lamb!

When the song was done, the place fell into
an eerie silence. Then Drover said, "Hank, do
you see what I see?"

"I'm afraid so. And did you hear what I just heard?"

"I'm afraid so."

"Have you ever heard that song before?"

"Yeah. Last night. Hank, do you believe in ghosts?"

"Affirmative."

"What?"

"Yes."

"What are we going to do now?"

The old man looked up from his hymn book and fixed his horrible bluish eyes on us. His right arm rose from his side and he pointed a finger at us. His lips moved and he said, "Dogs. D-O-G-S!"

And he started towards us—floating above the floor instead of walking.

The hair on my back shot up. "Drover, I don't know what you're going to do, but I'm fixing to build a new door in this cake house. See you around, son, it's every dog for himself!"

In my career as Head of Ranch Security, I have made a few claims that stretched the truth just a tiny bit. Yes, and I have exaggerated a few stories. But fellers, when I tell you that I by George ran smooth over that cake house door, you can put 'er down as 100% Guaranteed Truth. (See Guarantee of 100% Truth at end of book).

I did it, and if there had been five doors there instead of one, I would have taken out every one of them. The brethern and the sistren and the Followers of the Lamb might have been happy in that place, but it was time for this old dog to hunt some fresh air.

I didn't slow down or look back until I reached the house. Up ahead, I saw that Slim had just helped Miss Viola into the pickup and was about to close the door. I made a flying lap and landed right in her leap . . . flying leap and landed in her lap, I should say, and Drover was right behind me.

"What . . . where . . . why you crazy dogs, get out of that pickup!"

Did he think he was going to throw us out? Leave us there with that cake house full of ghosts and disturbed spirits?

No way.

There weren't enough winch trucks in Ochiltree County to drag me out of that pickup. When he tried to lift me out, I sank my claws into the seat covers and dug in.

"Why Slim," said Miss Viola, "these dogs act scared to death! Look at the way their hair is standing up. Why don't you let them ride up here with us. They'll be all right."

"Well . . . if you're sure they won't bother you."

He walked around to the other side, climbed in, and started the motor, and off we went to take Miss Viola home.

Slim looked down at me and laughed. " 'Smatter, Hankie, did them Halloween spooks get you mutts all stirred up?"

No. Well, maybe a little, at first.

"Well Hank, they were just the neighbors' kids, dressed up in costumes."

Yes, yes, we'd figgered that out.

"But you bought the whole program, thought they was creatures from the Black Lagoon!"

No, I'd thought nothing of the sort.

"Well, they got their candy and they've gone home, and we won't see spooks again for another year."

That's what he thought.

"You know, dogs are sure funny. One minute they'll do something that seems about half-way smart, and then they'll pull a stunt that makes you think they don't have any more brains than a rick of wood."

I laid my head across Miss Viola's lap and looked up into her eyes. She had a peculiar expression on her face, kind of serious, thoughtful. She wasn't laughing and making fun like some people I could mention.

She stroked me behind the ears, and for a long time she didn't say anything. Then, at last, she said, "Slim, these dogs are *really scared.* The hair hasn't gone down on their backs yet, and they're both shaking. It almost makes you think they'd seen . . . a ghost.''

"Nah, they're just typical ranch dogs, don't have sense enough to . . . you know, when I first moved into that place, one of the neigh-

G.L. Holmes

bors came over and told me some wild yarn about the cake house.''

"The cake house?''

"Yeah. He said back in the old days, it used to be a one room schoolhouse and they held church services in it on Sundays.''

"That's right,'' said Viola. "The old Alfalfa schoolhouse.''

"That's what he called it. He said they had a circuit-riding preacher many years ago, an old feller named John Dunham. One night at a revival service, he got so carried away, he just upped and died, and they buried him right out there behind the church.

"And what this neighbor told me was that every once in a while, old John Dunham comes back and tries to finish his revival service. I thought it was a pretty good story, myself, but of course I don't believe it.''

"You don't?''

"Heck no! Do you think I'd stay in that house if I thought there was a ghost around? I'd be gone so fast, he'd have to ride a fast horse to haunt me!'' There was a moment of silence. "I don't believe in ghosts, but I wouldn't want to live next door to one.''

We reached Viola's house. Slim left the motor running and got out to open her door. She took my head in both her hands and looked deep into my eyes.

"Hank," she whispered, "did you see old John Dunham's ghost tonight?" I whapped my tail against the floor. She smiled. "I think you did! And he scared the bejeebers out of you, didn't he?" I whapped my tail again, harder this time. "Slim would never believe that, but I do. I saw old John Dunham's ghost once when I was a little girl, and he scared the bejeebers out of me too."

Slim opened her door and waited for her to step out. She moved my head out of her lap and scratched me behind the ears. "You're a good dog, Hank. Thanks for helping me with supper."

She gave me a wink and then she was gone. I stood up on the seat and watched her go up the walk and up the steps. Just before she went inside, she turned and waved goodbye—*to me.*

I had the feeling that with just a little effort, I could fall head-over-heels in love with that old gal.

Slim climbed inside and we headed back to the place. He was feeling pretty good, smiling to himself and humming a song. When we bounced over the first cattle guard, he looked around at me.

"You ever see a lady who ate as much as that one? Boys, Miss Viola *loved* my Cowboy Round Steak! Next time, I'll have to double the recipe."

At that very moment, I burped. Pure garlic, from his famous Cowboy Round Steak.

When we got back to the place, Slim walked up to the door and closed his hand around the knob. He noticed that Mister Hide-on-the-Porch and I were poised and ready to shoot inside.

"Don't you dogs want to sleep in the cake house tonight? I believe if I was a dog I'd . . ."

But by then he'd already opened the door a crack, and that was all the space we needed. We were gone! We shot the gap, made a lightning dash back to the bedroom, dived into the bed, and crawled under the covers.

I dropped right off to sleep, but Drover wanted to talk.

"Hank, sometimes I get confused about what's real and what's not real. Do you reckon that was a real ghost we saw tonight?"

"Znork sprunk zizzifriss."

"Yeah, me too. I sure was scared."

"Zonkly sprinkling zordnipoof."

"Pete told us we'd see a ghost, and we sure did. Were you scared as bad as I was?"

"Zzzall I can tell you, Viola, is what I've zzzaid many timezzz before."

"My name's Drover. We left Viola at her house."

I opened my eyes and sat up. "Exactly, and you've just barged into a delicious dream I was having."

"Oh, 'scuse me. What was it you've told me many times before?"

"What are you talking about?"

"You were fixing to tell me something you've told me many times before."

"Oh, yes. Good night, Drover."

"That's all?"

"Good night, Drover, and shut your little trap."

"Oh. Good night, Hank."

"Good night, Drover."

"Good night."

"Good night."

"Nighty-night, Hank."

"Nighty shut up."

And with that, I pulled the rubber stopper of experience and listened as the bathwater of life went gurgling down the pipes of zzzzzzzzzzz zzzzzzzzzzzzzzzzzzzzzzzzzzzzzzzzzzzzzzzzzzzzzz zzzzzzzzzzzzzzzzzzzzzzzzzzzzzzzzzzzzzzzzzzzzzzzzz

GUARANTEE
OF
100% TRUTH

WHEREAS, my name is Hank the Cow-dog, and

WHEREAS, my name is not other than the aforementioned name named herewith, and

WHEREAS, I am certified as Head of Ranch Security, and

WHEREAS, I have served with distinction in that capacity for many aforementioned years, and

WHEREAS, Heads of Ranch Security are incapable of telling anything but 100% Truth, and

WHEREAS, there is nothing more to whereas or aforemention,

BE IT THEREFORE DISSOLVED THAT the story told by the Head of Ranch Security has been certified as 100% Truth, containing no fillers, dyes, or exaggerations.

Signed before me this day,

Hank the Cowdog

Head of Ranch Security
Truthee
Witnessether